Date: 6/27/11

**SP BR CAMARENA**
Camarena, Cathy,
Fey y Félix /

# Fey y Félix

**Cathy Camarena, M.Ed., and Gloria B. Ruff, M.Ed.**

**Consulting Editors**

Lourdes Flores-Hanson, M.S.E., and Gloria Rosso-White

Published by ABDO Publishing Company, 4940 Viking Drive, Edina, Minnesota 55435.

Printed in the United States.

Credits
Curriculum Coordinator: Nancy Tuminelly
Cover and Interior Design and Production: Mighty Media
Child Photography: Steven Wewerka, Wewerka Photography
Photo Credits: AbleStock, ShutterStock

Library of Congress Cataloging-in-Publication Data

Camarena, Cathy, 1966-
    Fey y Félix / Cathy Camarena, Gloria B. Ruff.
        p. cm. -- (Primeros sonidos)
    ISBN 1-59679-859-9 (hardcover)
    ISBN 1-59679-860-2 (paperback)
    1. Spanish language--Consonants--Juvenile literature. I. Ruff, Gloria B., 1971-
    II. Title. III. Series.
    PC4159.C349 2006
    468.1'3--dc22

                                                                    2005056906

SandCastle™ books are created by a professional team of educators, reading specialists, and content developers around five essential components that include phonemic awareness, phonics, vocabulary, text comprehension, and fluency. All books are written, reviewed, and leveled for guided and early intervention reading, and designed for use in shared, guided, and independent reading and writing activities to support a balanced approach to literacy instruction.

## Let Us Know

After reading the book, SandCastle would like you to tell us your stories about reading. What is your favorite page? Was there something hard that you needed help with? Share the ups and downs of learning to read. We want to hear from you! To get posted on the ABDO Publishing Company Web site, send us e-mail at:

**sandcastle@abdopub.com**

**SandCastle Level: Beginning**

ABCChDEFGH
IJKLLLMNÑOP
QRSTUVWXYZ

abcchdefgh
ijklllmnñop
qrstuvwxyz

**Fey**

**Félix**

**falda**

**foca**

**familia**

foco

feliz

Mira la .

Mira la  .

Mira la .

Este es un .

Él es .

Félix tiene una foca.

La foca tiene pelaje.

Fey tiene un foco.
El foco es blanco.

La foca tiene el foco.

El foco está en su nariz.

# ¿Cuáles de estas cosas comienzan con f?

# Más palabras que comienzan con f

farol

fecha

fuego

fuente

fútbol

23

# About SandCastle™

A professional team of educators, reading specialists, and content developers created the SandCastle™ series to support young readers as they develop reading skills and strategies and increase their general knowledge. The SandCastle™ series has four levels that correspond to early literacy development in young children. The levels are provided to help teachers and parents select the appropriate books for young readers.

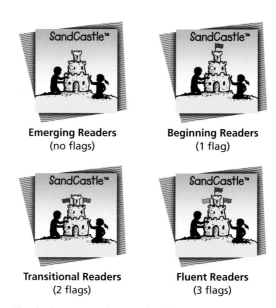

**Emerging Readers**
(no flags)

**Beginning Readers**
(1 flag)

**Transitional Readers**
(2 flags)

**Fluent Readers**
(3 flags)

These levels are meant only as a guide. All levels are subject to change.

To see a complete list of SandCastle™ books and other nonfiction titles from ABDO Publishing Company, visit **www.abdopub.com** or contact us at:

4940 Viking Drive, Edina, Minnesota 55435 • 1-800-800-1312 • fax: 1-952-831-1632